SOMETHING WILD

Molly Ruttan

 Nancy Paulsen Books

To my mother, Frances, who signed me up for violin lessons
when I was seven and went on to learn the viola for herself.

To SJ & Matt at the Silverlake Conservatory of Music
in Los Angeles, and to Linda, Doug, Phideaux, Gabe,
and my many fellow choir & bandmates over the years:
Thank you all for your amazing generosity of talent
and spirit, and for being a part of my musical journey,
onstage and off!

NANCY PAULSEN BOOKS

An imprint of Penguin Random House LLC, New York

First published in the United States of America by Nancy Paulsen Books,
an imprint of Penguin Random House LLC, 2023

Visit us online at penguinrandomhouse.com.

Library of Congress Cataloging-in-Publication Data is available.

Manufactured in China
ISBN 9780593112342
10 9 8 7 6 5 4 3 2 1
TOPL

Edited by Nancy Paulsen
Art direction by Cecilia Yung
Design by Suki Boynton
Text set in Cooper Old Style
The art was brought to life with charcoal,
pastel, acrylic paint, and digital media.

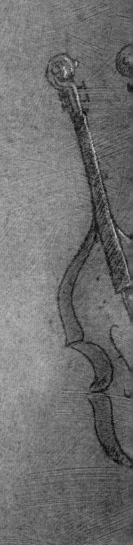

Ever since she was small, Hannah
loved to play her violin.

She loved the sound of it, and
she loved how it felt in her hands.

But she didn't love the idea of playing
in front of other people. AT ALL.

So when the day of the big recital arrived, Hannah was nervous.

When she thought about the huge audience, her legs trembled!

She secretly wished
something wild would happen . . .

so she wouldn't have to go!

But nothing wild happened.

It was almost time to leave.
Every time Hannah thought about
being onstage, her stomach lurched!
She felt a little queasy.

If only something wild would happen . . .

so she wouldn't
have to go!

But nothing wild happened.

They were almost at the school,
and Hannah's heart drummed in her chest.

She longed for something wild to happen . . .

so she wouldn't
have to go!

But nothing wild
happened . . .

nothing AT ALL.

The recital began.

Hannah was next.

Hannah walked onto the stage.
She saw the enormous audience.
Her stomach clenched,
    her legs wobbled,
        and her heart pounded.

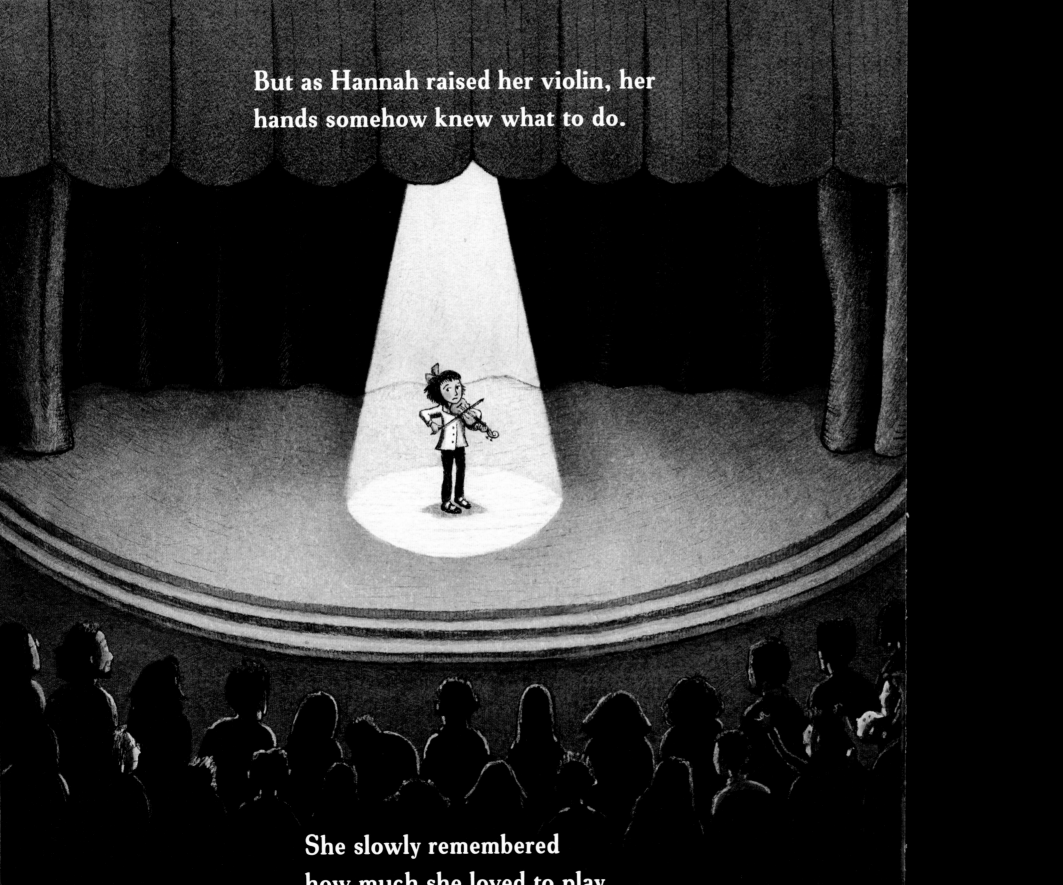

But as Hannah raised her violin, her
hands somehow knew what to do.

She slowly remembered
how much she loved to play

And that was when . . .

Something wonderfully . . .